PUFFIN

Recipe for
Disaster

PUFFIN BOOKS

Published by the Penguin Group
Penguin Books Ltd, 80 Strand, London WC2R 0RL, England
Penguin Group (USA) Inc., 375 Hudson Street, New York, New York 10014, USA
Penguin Group (Canada), 90 Eglinton Avenue East, Suite 700, Toronto, Ontario, Canada M4P 2Y3
(a division of Pearson Penguin Canada Inc.)
Penguin Ireland, 25 St Stephen's Green, Dublin 2, Ireland (a division of Penguin Books Ltd)
Penguin Group (Australia), 250 Camberwell Road, Camberwell, Victoria 3124, Australia
(a division of Pearson Australia Group Pty Ltd)
Penguin Books India Pvt Ltd, 11 Community Centre, Panchsheel Park, New Delhi – 110 017, India
Penguin Group (NZ), cnr Airborne and Rosedale Roads, Albany, Auckland 1310, New Zealand
(a division of Pearson New Zealand Ltd)
Penguin Books (South Africa) (Pty) Ltd, 24 Sturdee Avenue, Rosebank, Johannesburg 2196, South Africa

Penguin Books Ltd, Registered Offices: 80 Strand, London WC2R 0RL, England

www.penguin.com

First published 2006
1

www.bratzpack.com
Text TM and © MGA Entertainment, Inc. Bratz and all related logos, names,
characters and distinctive likenesses are the exclusive property of MGA Entertainment, Inc.
All Rights Reserved. Used under license by Puffin.

The moral right of the author has been asserted

Set in BeLucianBook by Palimpsest Book Production Limited, Polmont, Stirlingshire
Made and printed in England by Clays Ltd, St Ives plc

British Library Cataloguing in Publication Data
A CIP catalogue record for this book is available from the British Library

ISBN-13: 978-0-141-32148-6
ISBN-10: 0-141-32148-2

Recipe for
Disaster

By Zoe Fishman

PUFFIN

Other Bratz™ titles:

Chapter 1

"Hey, Cloe, wait up!" yelled Jade. Jade could see Cloe's ponytail weaving through the crowded hallway. Cloe turned around and broke into a smile when she saw Jade.

"Hurry up—I can't wait all day!" she teased. Jade caught up to her and gave her friend's ponytail a mischievous tug. "What's up? How's your day going?" she asked Cloe.

"Oh, it's fine," Cloe replied. "Except that it's Monday! I'm thinking I should've spent more time on homework and less on the phone yesterday—but somehow I never feel like it!"

"I totally hear you," Jade agreed. "And Monday is definitely the worst! Why does the weekend go so quickly?"

"I dunno, but it does fly by. So not fair!" said Cloe.

"We should see what we can do to change that," Jade said, grinning. "Stage a protest or something."

"Totally!" Cloe said, laughing. "We'll be the anti-Monday brigade, the most super-stylin' protesters ever!"

"What are you two up to?" asked Sasha as she and Yasmin strolled up to the others outside their classroom. "Looks like you're making trouble!"

"As usual," Yasmin added teasingly.

"It's true," Jade agreed. "You caught us."

"Hey, did you catch that show Ms. Shepard wanted us to watch?" asked Yasmin as they walked into their cooking class.

"Sure did," said Cloe. Their cooking teacher, Ms. Shepard, had asked the class to watch *Cooking with Louis Lyle* on Saturday afternoon. Louis Lyle was one of her favourite chefs and he was all over the scene—magazines, talk shows and charity events galore. He was *the* hot chef of the moment.

"I had no idea he was such a hottie!" whispered Cloe.

"Right?!" answered Jade excitedly. "He is too cute! And the food he was preparing looked delish! Like those sweet-potato pancakes—yum!"

"Oh yeah, I was totally salivating," added Cloe.

"Wait, that was the first time you girls had seen the show?" Yasmin asked. "Oh my gosh, it's like, my absolute favourite."

Looking dreamy, she continued, "In fact, I think he's inspired me to become a celebrity chef one day. Can't you just see me hosting my own show?"

"*Cooking with Yasmin?* Totally," Sasha said. "And hey, I can definitely see Chef Lyle's appeal—I mean, with that food and those looks, what's not to love?" The girls settled into their seats as their teacher made her way to the front of the classroom.

"Happy Monday, my little crumpets!" she

said. Jade looked at Sasha and giggled. Ms. Shepard loved using food words as terms of endearment. She was always calling them her "little tostadas" or "muffins", and it never failed to crack up the whole class. She had such an appreciation for food that she obviously couldn't get it off her mind.

"So, what did you think of Louis Lyle?" she asked coyly.

"Everything he made looked so delicious!" Yasmin blurted out. "Oops," she said, shooting her hand into the air.

"It's okay," said Ms. Shepard. "Go on."

"Well, it totally made me want to try all of his recipes," Yasmin said.

"I feel the same way!" Ms. Shepard agreed

enthusiastically. "And what did you think about his cooking style?" Ms. Shepard looked around the room for someone else to answer. "Yes, Kiana?" she asked.

"He's just super-accessible, you know?" Kiana said. "And he really makes cooking look easy and fun."

"Exactly!" exclaimed Ms. Shepard. "That's why I enjoy his show so much." Then, lowering her voice, she added, "Not to mention that he's easy on the eyes!" The girls in the class giggled while the boys rolled their eyes.

"But believe it or not, that's not the only reason I had you watch his show," said Ms. Shepard. "Yes, he makes cooking fun and he's one cute cookie, but guess what else?" The class watched her expectantly—she was even more worked up than usual, so they knew she had to be leading up to something big. Ms. Shepard paused for dramatic effect, then exclaimed, "He's coming here—to our very own class!" She was practically jumping up and down with excitement. Nearly every girl in the class squealed at the news.

"How cool is that?" Jade whispered. "A famous—not to mention way-cute—chef, right here at our school!"

"He'll probably make us something totally tasty, too," Cloe added. "I bet it'll be the most spectacular meal ever!"

"Shhh, shhh," Ms. Shepard said, calming the class down. "There's more! He's agreed to film one of his shows here—live!"

"That is so amazin'!" cried Sasha.

"But wait, I haven't told you the most 'amazin'" part yet," replied Ms. Shepard. "You'll all get to cook for him, and one lucky group will get to appear on the show he's taping here!" A buzz of excitement swept the room.

"Sign me up!" exclaimed Cloe.

"But wait, what do we have to do?" Sasha asked, always the practical one.

"I want you to break into groups of four and make me the tastiest lunch you can think of. Quiche or soufflé, dumplings or filet mignon, baked Brie or lobster bisque . . ." She trailed off, realizing that the whole class was staring at her while she was completely absorbed in her food fantasies. "Or, you know, whatever you think would be good," she finished quickly, sounding embarrassed. "You'll all serve your meals to both Louis and me, and he and I will pick the winners." She paused, clearly imagining a romantic meal with Louis Lyle before turning her attention to the class in front of her again. "Anyway, like I was saying, the group who cooks the most divine meal for us will get to prepare it side-by-side with Louis himself—live, on his show!" The class broke into excited chatter— even the boys were pumped at the chance to be on TV!

"Okay, class, go ahead and break into groups," Ms. Shepard instructed. "I want you to present me with a menu plan by the end of this class period—feel free to check out any of the books I have here for inspiration." She gestured to her huge bookcase, which covered an entire wall and was stuffed full of all sorts of cookbooks. "You'd better get moving—we only have forty-five minutes left this period!"

Cloe, Yasmin, Jade and Sasha immediately moved their desks together—of course they'd be a team—and, together, they knew they'd win!

Throughout the class, chairs skidded across the floor as everyone divided into teams. Nearby, Cameron, Eitan, Dylan and Koby formed one team, while their friends Kiana, Felicia, Phoebe and Siernna formed another, and Nevra, Dana, and twins Nona and Tess formed the fourth. The girls overheard Eitan say, "Guys, this is totally in the bag!" which made them laugh. They were crazy about their guy friends, but really, those boys didn't seem like the cooking type! Shaking their heads, the girls huddled to discuss their game plan.

"So, what do you guys think?" asked Jade.

"I think we should make something totally fancy," said Yasmin. "Maybe a soufflé, like Ms. Shepard suggested?"

"But aren't soufflés, like, totally hard to make?" Cloe protested. "What if it falls flat and all we have for Ms. Shepard and Chef Lyle to eat is a big pile of mush?"

"That's true . . . I've never actually made a soufflé before," Yasmin mused. "I've eaten a bunch of them, though, and let me tell you, they are *yummy*!"

"Right, but I'm not quite sure how that's going to help us in this particular case," Sasha said, "seeing as ours may not be so yummy if we have no clue how to make one."

"Hmm, good point," Yasmin agreed. "Well, then, something else fancy—I know, like a French Provençal feast!"

"Or what if we went the other way?" Jade suggested. "We could make something totally basic, like a chicken pot pie, but give it our own unique spin to really showcase our cooking skills."

"That could be really cool," Sasha replied, "but are you sure we really *have* cooking skills that good? Yeah, I make a tasty chicken salad sandwich, and Jade, I love your signature mac and cheese, and nothing beats Yasmin's nachos, but really, creating a whole new recipe—I mean, that's like what Louis Lyle does himself!"

"Geez, Sasha, are you saying you don't believe in our culinary abilities?" Jade asked. When Sasha started to protest, Jade added, "Sash, I'm totally kidding. You're right—we aren't exactly celebrity chefs."

But Sasha was barely listening—it was clear she'd been struck with a fabulous new idea. "You guys," she said, "why don't we prepare one of his signature dishes? It'll be like a tribute to him, and he'll be totally impressed if we do it right."

"And his recipes are all so spectacular, it'll be a breeze to make something totally delish!" Yasmin chimed in.

"Sounds great to me," Jade agreed. "So let's grab his cookbooks and take our pick!"

Ms. Shepard was strolling through the classroom, making sure everyone was actually working instead of just chatting with their friends, and overheard this last comment. "Sorry, girls, but as hard as it is to believe, I don't have every cookbook ever made on those shelves over there. And Louis Lyle is such a hot new chef, I haven't gotten the school to order me copies of his yet." She leaned in and added conspiratorially, "But I'm hoping he'll give me a complete set when he comes to visit—maybe even signed!"

The girls tried not to show their disappointment. "That's cool, Ms. Shepard,"

Cloe said. "Thanks for saving us the trouble of searching the entire shelf, anyway." Ms. Shepard nodded and headed off to check on their classmates. The girls watched her go, then let out a collective moan.

"*What* are we going to *do?*" Cloe cried, shedding her calm demeanour of moments before. "That was the perfect idea, and now there's no way we can do it—not if we have to turn in our menu by the end of class!" She slumped over her desk and moaned, "This is *so* unfair!"

"Wait, Cloe, I think it'll be okay," Yasmin interrupted.

"How can it *possibly* be okay?" Cloe wailed, in full drama-queen mode.

"Like I told you, I watch his show every

week," she said. "And a few weeks ago he had on some big-time actress, and he made her a curried-chicken salad sandwich on freshly baked pumpernickel bread. He said it was the perfect dish to make a lunch feel special without being too fussy."

"Is that a direct quote?" Jade asked, and when Yasmin nodded seriously, they all burst into giggles.

"Girl, you have been hiding a real obsession here!" Sasha teased.

"What?" Yasmin squealed, blushing. "I just really like his cooking, you know?"

"Mmm-hmm," Cloe said. "I'm *sure* it's just his cooking you like!"

"Hey, you guys all said he was totally hot

too," Yasmin protested. "So I just have first dibs, that's all!"

"Ladies, focus here," said Sasha. "We can tease Yas about her Louis fixation later. But, right now, we have to get this menu nailed down! Class is almost over, and we haven't decided anything yet!"

"Sorry," said Jade. "You're right."

Sasha turned her notebook to a fresh sheet of paper and uncapped her pen. "Okay, Yasmin's chicken salad idea sounds great—and you know that *is* my personal specialty, so I think that'll help. I mean, I can totally take the lead on making that, so we know that'll be perfect."

"Cuz obviously anything you do will be perfect, right, Sash?" Jade said, rolling her eyes.

"Um, *yeah*," Sasha said, laughing. "No, really, girls, I know the whole thing will be perfect because we'll be making it together!"

"Awww," the other girls cooed—then burst into giggles.

"Okay, so Sasha's on chicken salad—and maybe we should finish off with my famous cupcakes?" Cloe suggested.

"Mmm, yeah, those'll blow him away!" Jade agreed. "Ooh, and I'll make my signature strawberry smoothies."

"Perfect!" Yasmin agreed. "Well, since the pumpernickel bread is supposed to be the hardest part, and I *am* the one who saw the show, I'll take care of that."

"Plus Louis will be impressed if he knows

you made his gourmet bread all by yourself, right, Yas?" Cloe added.

"Well, maybe . . ." Yasmin admitted.

"Hey, if Yas wants to take on the hardest part, I'm all for it!" Jade exclaimed. "I mean, I know I couldn't do it!"

"Totally," Sasha agreed. She noticed Cloe doodling on her sketch pad. "Whatcha got there, Angel?"

"Oh, I was just writing up our menu," Cloe replied. She turned her pad so the other girls could see the beautiful menu she'd designed. She'd written "A Lovely Luncheon for Louis Lyle" across the top in gorgeous calligraphy. Below that, it said:

Menu

Main Course

Louis's Own Curried-Chicken Salad

served on fresh-baked pumpernickel bread

—prepared by Sasha & Yasmin

Beverages

Jade's Scrumptious Strawberry Smoothies

Dessert

Cloe's Divine Vanilla Cupcakes

with buttercream frosting

She had embellished the edges with scrolling vines and flowers. It looked amazin'!

"Cloe, that's gorgeous!" Sasha exclaimed. "It looks just like a real menu at a fancy restaurant! Ms. Shepard is gonna be totally impressed."

"Yeah, if our food tastes as good as that looks, we'll win for sure!" Jade added.

Just then, Ms. Shepard clapped her hands to get their attention. "Class, if you haven't already given me your menus, please turn them in now," she announced. The girls looked around and were startled to see that they were the only ones who were still working! They scrambled over to the teacher's desk to turn in their menu.

"This looks lovely, girls," she said. "Okay, everyone's menus sound great. Now for next class, bring these meals, fully prepared, so Chef Lyle and I can enjoy them. And come hungry too—I don't know about Louis, but I know I can't eat four lunches by myself!"

Her students laughed, and just then the

bell rang. Everyone scurried to gather their things, but Yasmin hung back at Ms. Shepard's desk.

"Yes, Yasmin, did you have a question?" the teacher asked.

"It's just, I'm worried about our pumpernickel bread," Yasmin explained. "I know from watching Chef Lyle make it on his show that it's really important that it be fresh from the oven, but if we make it the night before, it won't be," she explained. "And I'm just afraid it won't taste good enough!"

"Well I must say I'm glad to see you taking your cooking so seriously," Ms. Shepard said. "I'll tell you what—I'll write you a pass to get out of your morning classes that day, and you can come straight here and start baking. How long would you need?"

"Well, he said on the show it takes about four hours to give it enough time to rise and everything," Yasmin replied.

"Well then, report here first thing in the morning, and you can bake away all day!" Ms. Shepard exclaimed. "I'll have other classes, but they can work around you!"

"Oh, Ms. Shepard, that would be fabulous," Yasmin squealed. "You're the coolest!" She dashed out of the room to tell the others the news, and almost ran over them—they were standing right outside the door, looking totally down.

"What's the deal, girls?" she asked. "We just

came up with a fabulous menu, and Ms. Shepard even agreed to let me out of my other classes so I can bake the bread that morning so it'll be all warm and fresh and perfect!"

"That's cool, Yas," Sasha said, "but we just remembered, we still don't have the recipes, and we need to go grocery shopping and do a trial run before our next class, and there just isn't enough time!"

Just then, Kiana joined them in the hallway. The girls hadn't even noticed that she was still in the classroom, so they were startled to see her appear at their side.

"Hey, girls," she said. "What's happenin'?"

"Oh, nothing . . . we're just trying to figure out how we'll have the time to get everything together for the big cook-off," Cloe explained. "We really wanna win!"

"Yeah, us too," Kiana replied. "Luckily, my family cooks all the time at home, so I have pretty much all of the ingredients already, plus the recipes of course."

"See that's the problem," Yasmin chimed in. "We wanted to make one of Louis's signature dishes, but we don't own a Louis Lyle cookbook!"

"Oh, we have all of his books at home," Kiana said. "I can bring you one tomorrow if you want. Just let me know which recipe you're looking for."

"Really?" Sasha said. "That would be super-cool if you'd let us borrow it!"

"You won't try to steal our idea, will you?" Jade teased.

"Nah, our menu is pretty solid," Kiana shot back. "We're ready to take on whatever you dish out!"

"Okay then," Sasha replied. "We wanted to make his curried-chicken salad and pumpernickel bread. Do you think you have those recipes?"

"For sure!" Kiana replied. "Those are stellar picks, girls! Guess we'll have some stiff competition, huh?"

"That's the plan!" Cloe agreed, laughing.

Chapter 2

After school that day, the girls met up to finalize their game plan. They were determined to get that spot on Louis Lyle's show!

"Are you *sure* we can't get the recipes from Kiana tonight?" Cloe asked. "I'm totally stressed that we won't have time to try them out before Ms. Shepard does!"

"No, she had a drama rehearsal today, and she won't be back till late," Sasha reminded them. "But we can make *my* special chicken salad, just in case."

"Maybe we should," Jade agreed. "I mean,

how different can one chicken salad be from another? At least then we'll already have most of the ingredients we need."

"Hey, no complaints here," Yasmin added. "I'm always up for some of Sasha's yummy chicken salad! Cloe, are you sure you don't need to test out your cupcakes too?"

"Nah . . . but you're right, we could go ahead and buy everything we need for those," Cloe replied.

"And for my smoothies!" Jade said.

"Totally," Sasha agreed. "Girls, we're gonna be fine."

"Correction," Yasmin said. "We're gonna be awesome!"

The girls split up to grab their own recipes at home, and met up at the supermarket to shop. Sasha, as usual, was the first to arrive.

"Hey, Bunny Boo!" she heard from behind her. She turned around to see Jade approaching, smiling and waving.

"Hey, Kool Kat!" Sasha replied. "Are you ready to take this grocery store by storm?"

"Totally!" said Jade. "We are totally going to rock at this. Louis Lyle will be blown away!"

"Hey, girls!" called Cloe and Yasmin, approaching from the other direction.

"Okay, now that we're all here, let's get a move on!" Sasha exclaimed. "Did you all bring your recipes?" Her friends nodded, handing them over. "Awesome," she said. "I'll divide up the ingredients so we can jet through the store, and then we'll meet back here at the front." She whipped out her notebook, and quickly jotted down separate lists for each of them, then handed them out. "Sound good?"

"Totally!" the girls exclaimed. They each grabbed a shopping cart and darted to separate corners of the store.

Cloe scoped out her list. "Okay," she said to herself. "Chicken, celery, eggs, water chestnuts . . . I can do that." She manoeuvred her way down the aisles to the meat section. "Okay, chicken— got it." But wait, she thought, looking at the rows of various types of chicken in front of her. Bones or no bones? With skin or without? She didn't know what to pick! She felt herself starting to freak out, and looked around to see if there was anyone who could help her.

"Hey, Cloe, what's wrong?" she heard a familiar voice ask. She turned to find Eitan standing beside her.

"Oh hey!" Cloe exclaimed. "What are you doing here?"

"Probably the same thing you are," said Eitan. "Getting stuff for our cooking class."

"Oh, are the other boys here too?" She looked around, and Eitan laughed.

"No, Cameron's not here," he said. Everyone knew Cloe and Cam were crushin' on each other, but neither of them would ever make a move. They cared too much about their friendship to do that.

Blushing, Cloe stammered, "No—I wasn't asking about Cam specifically, I was just—"

"Whatever, Cloe," Eitan said with a grin. "But now back to the business at hand. Why does all this poultry have you lookin' so puzzled?"

"Because there's just so *much* of it!" Cloe wailed. "All I want is some plain old chicken, and I don't even know which one that is!"

"Dude, chill," said Eitan. "I would be happy to guide you through the wonderful world of chicken."

"Seriously?" Cloe asked. "But you're on a different team!"

"Yeah, but we're still friends, silly," he replied. "And anyway, we're totally not threatened by you."

"Oh really?" Cloe demanded jokingly. "Well let me tell you, you should be!"

"Right, as soon as you get out of the poultry aisle, watch out!" Eitan teased.

"We'll just have to see," Cloe said. "But in the meantime, are you gonna help me pick some chicken or not? Cuz Sasha's got us on a schedule, and you know coming between Sasha and her plans is so not a good idea!"

"Yeah, she'll come after me if I keep you any longer!" Eitan agreed. "Okay, so what exactly are you making with this chicken?" Cloe looked at him suspiciously, and he continued, "Look, there's no way I can tell you what to get if you don't tell me what it's for—I'm not exactly a chicken psychic, you know."

"Okay . . ." Cloe said. She wondered if Sasha would be mad if yet another team found out what they were making. But when she turned to look at the wall of chicken again, she knew she had no choice. She took a deep breath and said, "We're making chicken salad. So what kind of chicken is that?"

"White meat, boneless," he said right away. "Here's the one." He grabbed the package and handed it over.

"Man, you really know your way around a grocery store!" she said. "And I thought you guys would have it tougher, what with being an all-boy team."

"Hey, I make sandwiches at the smoothie bar," Eitan protested. "And anyway, my parents and I all love to cook together. I've been cooking since I was a little kid."

"Wow, that's awesome!" Cloe exclaimed. "Guess you're the guy to beat then, huh?"

"I sure am," Eitain said with a grin. "Catch ya later, Cloe," he called as he strolled away.

Chapter 3

The girls lugged all their shopping bags into Sasha's house, dumped them in her kitchen, then crashed in the living room.

"Ugh, this is why I never cook," Jade moaned from the couch. "It's way too much work!"

"But for the chance to cook side-by-side with Louis Lyle, there's no such thing as too much work!" Yasmin said, bouncing up and down on Sasha's cushy chair. "Aren't you guys totally pumped?"

"Yeah, we're pumped," said Cloe sleepily.

"But since we still don't have the recipes, can we please go home? I have an essay due tomorrow that I haven't even started."

"Oh my gosh, me too!" Yasmin cried. "Okay, let's get outta here—but tomorrow, it's all about the baking, right?"

"Totally," the other girls agreed.

* * *

The next morning at school, they were utterly beat. Sasha was barely keeping her eyes open in her first hour when Kiana rushed in, waving two recipe cards triumphantly. "Here they are!"

Startled, Sasha jerked fully awake. "Geez, girl, it's too early in the morning for that much energy!"

"Oh, sorry—" Kiana began, but Sasha interrupted.

"No, *I'm* sorry—it's not your fault I'm not a morning person!" Sasha said. "Seriously, thank you so much for bringing these for us." She read over the index cards, where Kiana had neatly printed each recipe. "Mmm, these sound *good*!"

"I know, right?" agreed Kiana. "Almost made me wish I *could* steal your idea—but of course, I'd never do that," she added hurriedly.

"Of course," Sasha replied, still reading through the recipes. "Wow, this bread is gonna be hard—I hope we don't screw it up!"

"I totally believe in you," said Kiana.

"Aw, thanks man," Sasha said. "Good luck tomorrow, for real."

"You too," Kiana replied. "And may the best bakers win!"

* * *

At the grocery store that night, official recipes in hand, the girls hit the aisles once again to pick up the missing ingredients. Jade got the baked goods aisle, and almost immediately found herself as mixed up as Cloe had been with the chicken the night before. "Wholewheat flour? Cracked wheat flour? Brown rice flour? Man, who knew there were so many different types of flour in the world?" she muttered, frustrated.

"Who ya talkin' to, Kool Kat?" a boy's voice asked behind her. Jade whirled to see Eitan grinning at her.

"Oh—uh—I was just tryin' to figure out

what the heck all these crazy flour varieties are," she explained. "There are, like, ten different kinds in this recipe!"

"I thought you were making chicken salad," he said. "Are you sure you need flour for that?"

"No, no, it's for the pumpernickel bread to go *with* the chicken salad," she said, then paused, narrowing her eyes at him. "Hey wait, how'd you know what we were making?"

"Oh, Cloe told me yesterday," he replied.

"Why would she do that?" Jade demanded.

"Jade, c'mon, it was nothing," he protested. "I was just helping her find the right chicken, and—"

"You were here at the same time as us yesterday too?" Jade asked.

"Yeah, so what?" he demanded.

"Chill, Eitan," Jade replied. "Just seems like a pretty big coincidence, doesn't it?"

"I don't think so," he said defensively. "Anyway, do you want my help decoding the flour or not?"

"Dude, I'm sorry. Here you're trying to help us, and I'm like jumping all over you," Jade said, embarrassed. "I guess I'm just totally stressed by this grocery store—it's like, way too many choices!"

"It's cool—I mean, getting to meet dreamy Louis Lyle *is* a pretty big prize," he said, batting his eyelashes and making Jade burst out in giggles. "Seriously, I mean yeah, you're like the competition, but Ms. Shepard *did* say we'd all get to eat everything, so it helps me too if yours is as tasty as possible, right?"

"True," Jade agreed. "I hadn't thought of it that way. Okay, so what delish meal are you making for us?"

"Uh-uh, that's a secret," he said.

"No fair!" Jade squealed. But Eitan was already pulling bags of flour off the shelves and loading them into her cart, and she was so relieved not to have to work it out herself that she figured she'd better stop complaining.

Chapter 4

Sasha's kitchen was a total disaster area. Flour, soy sauce and sugar were strewn everywhere—even in the girls' hair—and it looked like every pot and pan in the house had been used in the preparations.

"Wow, can you imagine what it would look like if we'd made the bread?" Cloe asked, shaking her head in amazement.

"But are you sure you'll have enough time tomorrow, Yasmin?" Sasha asked, worried. "And will you be able to manage all by yourself?"

"It'll be fine," Yasmin replied. "Remember, I

am a true Louis Lyle devotee. I am all over this bread recipe!"

"Fabulous," Cloe said. "Now, how 'bout a taste test of everything else?"

"I could go for a cupcake right about now!" Yasmin said, snagging one from the pretty platter on the counter. "Tast-ee!" she declared around a mouthful of cupcake.

"Oooh, this chicken salad is outta this world," Jade said, sneaking a quick forkful.

"So far, so good," Sasha said. "Jade, wanna pour me a smoothie?"

"My pleasure," Jade replied, filling up a glass for her friend. Sasha took a sip and smiled. "Delicious as usual!" she announced. "Now, it's all up to you, Yasmin."

"No prob," Yasmin said, but she couldn't help feeling nervous—she'd never baked her own bread before, and she wouldn't have any time to fix it if it came out wrong. She'd barely get it finished in time for class even if everything went perfectly!

* * *

The next morning, Sasha's alarm shrieked in her ear. She shot up in bed, completely flustered. She turned off the alarm and sighed, rubbing her eyes. Today was the day they would meet Louis Lyle and she had hardly slept a wink! She and the girls had stayed up late chatting, and then she'd spent all night tossing and turning, thinking about the big day. She had even had a nightmare where she was attacked by a giant rising loaf of bread. It had reached such a height that it had taken over the entire kitchen, and the refrigerator and stove had been submerged in dough! She'd had to run as fast as she could to avoid the same fate. Sasha couldn't help but laugh, remembering it now, but it had been totally scary the night before!

She checked the clock. She had decided to wake up early so she could cart all of the food and supplies to school for the set-up. She stretched and rolled out of bed. *First things first—I have got to look fabulous!* she thought. She surveyed the contents of her closet. She needed to look cool but professional. *You never know,* she thought, *Louis Lyle could be secretly scouting for a new assistant!* She giggled as she imagined herself on his show, chopping vegetables and trading witty barbs with Louis. "The Louis and Sasha Show!" she said aloud, trying it out. From her closet, she pulled a black skirt and her latest purchase, a seriously stylish velvet blazer. She wrinkled her nose as she searched her shoe selection. She selected a pair of round-toe black flats. She brushed her hair and styled it in a sleek bun. *Perfect!* she thought, surveying herself in the mirror.

She glanced at the clock. "Yikes!" she said—she only had a half hour to grab the food and supplies and make it to school. Luckily, she had compiled a checklist the night before so she wouldn't forget anything. She grabbed the list and her school bag and headed downstairs to the kitchen.

"Okay, salad—check," she said to herself as she pulled it from the refrigerator. It really did look amazing. She crossed "salad" off her list. "Smoothies, check!" she added, pulling a large, watertight thermos out of the fridge as well. "Cupcakes, check!" she continued, retrieving them from the counter where they'd been left to cool. Then she piled all of the bread ingredients into a shopping bag, checking them off on the recipe card as she went. "Bread, check!" she said as she drew another line through her list.

She had decided to bring pretty plates and silverware as well. Louis Lyle was big on presentation and there was no way she was going to serve him their gourmet meal on paper plates!

Before wrapping them carefully in tissue paper, she pulled the plates and silverware from their cabinets and crossed "place settings" off her list. *What else?* she thought. *Oh yeah, linen napkins!* She added them to her bag as well.

"Did you pack glasses?" Jade asked, appearing in Sasha's kitchen. The girls were so close that they just walked in and out of each others' houses as casually as if they were their own, and they'd agreed to meet up this morning before school cuz there was no way Sasha could carry all this herself!

"Ooh, good catch, Jade," Sasha replied, pulling two nice glasses out of the cabinet. "I should grab a stylish pitcher for your smoothies too!" She turned to really look at Jade, and grinned—Kool Kat looked amazin' in a leopard-print jacket and jeans.

"Check you out!" Sasha exclaimed.

"Hey, I had to make an effort for Chef Cutie," Jade said, and they both laughed.

"I'm here, I'm here," Cloe cried, rushing in. "Sorry I'm late!"

"It's okay, you're just in time," Sasha replied. "*And* you're lookin' cute!" she added, taking in Cloe's slim-fitting, chocolate corduroy blazer.

"Why thank you," Cloe said, doing a little twirl. "You're lookin' pretty fab yourself!"

"Okay, girls, we can finish admiring each others' fashion sense later," Jade said. "But for now, we better get all this to Yasmin so she can get bakin'!" The girls had decided to just meet

Yasmin at the school, cuz they figured she'd be stressed enough with all the work she'd have to do that morning, without having to make an extra stop on her way there.

"C'mon, girls, let's ride!" Cloe exclaimed, and they all hurried out the door, their arms full of bags and packages.

* * *

Yasmin, in the meantime, woke up late that morning, and had to scramble to get to school in time. The girls met her at their cooking classroom and handed over all the bread ingredients. They did have to laugh when they saw that she too had gone for the glam-professional look, in a wide-sleeved shrug with a flower pin on the lapel.

"Wow, guess you got the dress-code memo too," Jade said, grinning.

"Hey, what can I say—great minds think alike!" Yasmin replied.

Cloe loaded their smoothies and salad into the class fridge, while Jade lined up the bread ingredients on the counter, and Sasha gave Yasmin a little pep talk.

"Good luck, Pretty Princess," she said. "I know you can do it!"

"Thanks, Sash," Yasmin said. "I sure hope so!"

Chapter 5

After the girls left, Yasmin stared at the recipe card, determined to do everything perfectly. There were an awful lot of steps, and it wasn't nearly as much fun without all her girls gathered around, cracking her up and making the time fly by. But soon she was so busy, pouring and mixing and checking on the loaves that she hardly even noticed how long it had been, and she was surprised when the girls suddenly appeared beside her.

"Well?" Sasha asked. "How is it?"

"I haven't even gotten to try it yet!" Yasmin

cried, pushing her hair back and smearing flour all across her face in the process. "Oh man, Louis will be here any minute, huh?" The girls nodded, and Yasmin looked terrified.

"Babe, go get cleaned up," Sasha said. "I'll pull the bread out of the oven for you, okay? You're just waiting for the timer to go off, right?"

"Yeah, it's just got a couple minutes left," Yasmin agreed. "And since we wanted to serve it warm, it's perfect if it comes out of the oven right before he gets here."

"Awesome!" Jade said. "Yas, you totally did it!"

"Yeah, we'll see how awesome I am when I taste it," Yasmin replied glumly.

"Why, did something go wrong?" Cloe asked.

"No, it's just my favourite chef ever is going to be eating my bread, and I don't even know if it's any good! It just makes me a little nervous, you know?" Yasmin explained.

"Totally," Cloe said. "But I'm sure it'll be fabulous, cuz you made it, and you're fabulous!" She gave Yasmin a hug, and Yas smiled at her friend gratefully. "C'mon, let's go get you ready to meet the chef of your dreams!" Cloe and Yasmin darted to the bathroom for some last-minute primping, while Sasha and Jade stood watch over the oven. Moments later, the classroom had filled up, the bread was waiting on the countertop, and Yasmin reappeared, looking totally glam with her hair cascading in long layers down her back and a touch of shimmer on her eyelids and lips.

"Girl, you are gonna blow that chef away!" Jade squealed.

"Would I be the chef in question?" Louis Lyle asked, strolling into the room with Ms. Shepard scurrying excitedly after him.

"Um, yes you would," Cloe said, trying to cover for Yasmin as her cheeks turned bright red. "We were just, you know, talking about how much we think you'll like the yummy lunch we made for you!"

"Wonderful!" Louis said. "That sounds good to me. Let's start with yours!" The girls looked at each other nervously, but they were really excited too—he seemed just as cool in person as he had on his show, and they could hardly believe he was about to eat stuff they'd made!

Chef Lyle and Ms. Shepard settled at a table in the middle of the room while the class watched eagerly. Cloe laid a hand-lettered copy of their menu in front of each of them, and arranged silverware and napkins alongside. Jade poured them each a tall glass of strawberry smoothie, and Yasmin placed the bread loaves in a chic bread basket and set it in front of them. Sasha scooped chicken salad on to a large lettuce leaf on each plate, making sure the presentation looked totally tasty, then laid each plate in front of them. Cloe set cupcakes on cute little dessert plates at the edge of the table.

"This table is, like, straight out of a magazine!" marvelled Yasmin as they all stood around admiring it.

"For real," whispered Jade.

"I'm so proud of us!" Sasha squealed. She'd been sure they could do it if they all worked together!

"Yes, girls, very good presentation. Now, why don't you introduce yourselves to Chef Lyle, and tell him about your menu?" Ms. Shepard instructed.

Jade, never shy, spoke up right away. "I'm Jade, and I made the delish strawberry smoothies you're about to enjoy."

"And I'm Sasha, and I prepared your curried-chicken salad recipe, Chef Lyle," Sasha said.

"Please, call me Louis," the chef interjected, and the girls exchanged grins. He was a total sweetie! They were starting to feel less nervous already.

"Well, I'm Yasmin, and it's, like, a huge honour to have you here. I am *such* a huge fan of yours," Yasmin babbled. "Oh, right, and I made the bread."

"And I made the cupcakes!" Cloe added. "So you better start eating so you'll have time to get to them!"

"Now *that* is good advice," Louis said, laughing. "What do you say, Ms. Shepard?" he asked, turning to their teacher. "Shall we?"

"Yes, please, dig in!" Ms. Shepard said, giving him a huge smile.

"I think I'll start with the chicken salad by itself," he said as though he were narrating his cooking show. "It's fantastic with the bread too, but I also love to enjoy its flavour all by itself."

The class murmured agreement as if he'd said something really profound. He scooped up a forkful of chicken salad, and closed his eyes happily.

"Girls, this is delicious!" he exclaimed. "It has just the right mix of sweet and spicy—the curry gives it a kick but isn't overpowering. Great job!" Ms. Shepard was nodding along with every word he said.

They both took sips of their smoothies, and Ms. Shepard cooed, "Jade, this is positively sublime." The girls grinned—it was going perfectly!

Then Chef Lyle pulled off a chunk of the

bread, and the girls held their breath—who knew if it had come out right? But as he tugged, instead of pulling away like a normal piece of bread, the whole chunk crumbled in his hand.

"Is it supposed to do that?" Cloe whispered anxiously. "I don't think it's supposed to do that!"

Yasmin looked mortified, but Sasha stepped forward. "We thought it would be a cool take on it to go with more of a breadcrumb thing," she said. "Just crumble it over your chicken salad, and mix it on in!"

"What a creative idea!" Ms. Shepard cried. She reached for the bread basket, grabbed a handful of crumbs, and sprinkled them over her chicken salad. Chef Lyle did the same, and as they both raised their forks to their mouths, the girls grabbed each others' hands and squeezed tight. They already knew the bread wasn't exactly right—but how would it taste?

"Mmmm," Louis said. "I must say, I never would have thought of approaching this menu quite this way, but it totally works, girls! Well done."

Yasmin heaved a huge sigh of relief as the other girls pulled her into a hug. She'd been so scared that she'd messed everything up somehow! Ms. Shepard and Chef Lyle gobbled up their cupcakes, and agreed that those were totally divine. The girls couldn't stop grinning—their meal was a success!

But now the other groups had to go, and who knew if they'd be better? The boys volunteered to go next, and totally impressed the judges with a truly tasty stew. Then another group presented the pair with a spinach quiche. And Kiana's group finished off with lasagne. After they'd eaten everything, Ms. Shepard and Louis went into the teacher's office to discuss the teams, inviting the students to eat up while they waited.

"Wow, this *is* really great," Kiana said, trying the chicken salad with breadcrumbs. "How'd you get the idea to do it like this?"

"Oh, um, it just kind of struck me," Yasmin replied as her best friends tried to hide their smiles. "And, Kiana, your lasagne is totally yummy too."

"Hey, try out our stew!" Dylan demanded. "It totally rocks!"

"Yeah, that's some good stuff," Jade agreed, digging in.

"And your quiche is fabulous too," Cloe told Dana. "I guess we all really made it tough on our judges, huh?"

As the others nodded, Louis Lyle and Ms. Shepard strode back into the room. "Well, class, it wasn't easy, but we have decided on a winner." She paused for dramatic effect, then exclaimed, "Joining Louis on his show to be taped here tomorrow are Cloe, Yasmin, Jade and Sasha!"

"Oh my gosh!" Cloe squealed, leaping into the air. The girls launched themselves into a group hug, jumping up in down with excitement.

"Your presentation was amazing, from the

gorgeous menu cards to the salad's arrangement on the plate. And I loved that you prepared a full meal, not just one course," Louis gushed. "And I'm so impressed that you could create a tasty new take on one of my very own dishes! However did you come up with the idea?"

Yasmin pulled herself out of the group hug, looking sheepish. She knew she could never lie to her fave chef. She sighed and said very softly, "We didn't."

"Yasmin, what are you saying?" Ms. Shepard demanded. "Are you trying to tell me this was the result of some cooking error?"

"It must've been," Yasmin said. "I mean, I thought I followed the recipe exactly, but it didn't come out right! I'm so sorry," she said, holding back tears and trying not to look at the chef she admired so much.

"As delectable as it was, I can't reward careless cooking," Ms. Shepard said. "I'm sorry, girls, but I'm going to have to declare the boys' team the winner instead."

"Wait, Ms. Shepard," Sasha said. "If we can prove it wasn't Yasmin's fault, can we still have the slot?"

"Of course," Ms. Shepard said, "but I just don't see how—"

"Leave it to us," Jade interrupted. "We'll get to the bottom of this!"

Chapter 6

When the girl's arrived at Yasmin's house after school, she was practically in tears. "I feel so terrible for blowing our chance," she wailed. "I just don't understand what could've happened!"

"Okay, let's work backwards," said Sasha, taking the lead as usual. "You're sure you followed the recipe card word for word?"

"Of course!" Yasmin cried. "You know how important this is to me! I checked every ingredient twice before I put it in!"

"But you were really tired this morning,"

Cloe reminded her. "Are you sure you didn't get mixed up?"

"Totally sure," Yasmin said. "Everything that went in that bowl was exactly what the recipe said!"

"Okay, so if it wasn't Yasmin, what if we brought her the wrong ingredients?" Jade asked.

"No way—I checked and double-checked—you saw my list this morning!" Sasha replied.

"That's not quite what I meant," Jade said. "I should've told you guys, but, well, there were so many different kinds of flour for that recipe that I got totally confused, and then I ran into Eitan, and he seemed to know all about baking, and I just let him load the flour into my cart. I mean, this doesn't seem like him, but he *was* acting kinda weird, and I don't know, maybe he switched one of the labels or something to mix us up?"

"But why would he do that?" Yasmin cried. "He knew how pumped we were about meeting Louis Lyle!"

"Yeah, but he really wanted to win too," Cloe said thoughtfully. "And actually, when he helped me pick out the chicken he was acting sort of strange too. But there was nothing wrong with the chicken salad, so that doesn't make sense."

"Nothing wrong *that we know of*," Sasha said darkly.

"Oh come on," Jade said. "We'd definitely have noticed if the chicken was off."

"Okay, but you might really be on to

something with this flour thing," Sasha said. "But how do we find out if he did it?"

Cloe looked from Sasha's angry face to Yasmin's teary one, and she got mad too. "That's it, I'm calling Cam," she declared. "I'll have him bring Eitan and meet me at the coffee shop in an hour. And don't worry, I'll get it out of him."

* * *

When the boys arrived to meet Cloe, they looked totally nervous.

"Look, we're really sorry about what happened with your bread," Cam said right away. "And it totally sucks that we ended up getting the TV spot instead of you. We'd give it back to you if we could."

"But we can't," Eitan added. "It's not up to us!"

"And you sounded way upset on the phone," Cam added. "So c'mon, Cloe—what is this all about?"

"Well, Eitan, I don't want to offend you," Cloe began, "but—well—you were definitely involved in the ingredient buying for our team— in fact you kept showing up everywhere we turned—and it *is* your team that benefited from this mix-up. So, we were just wondering, well ..."

"Are you seriously asking if I sabotaged you?" Eitan demanded.

"Yeah, Cloe, I know you're upset about the cook-off, but that's out of line," Cameron said.

"Really?" Cloe asked. "So Eitan told you he picked out all the flour we used in that bread, not to mention the chicken I got for the chicken salad?"

"You did?" Cameron asked, surprised.

"What were you doing grocery shopping for another team?"

"Probably spying on us!" Cloe exclaimed.

"No—that wasn't it," Eitan said. "Look, I didn't want to say anything but ... well, I'm really into cooking, so this was a big deal to me too. I really wanted to be in a group with you girls, cuz I know how great you always do at whatever you try. But I knew you four would work together, so I went with the boys." He looked at Cameron sheepishly. "Sorry, man—no disrespect to you."

"No worries, it's cool," Cam said, shrugging. "I mean, who wouldn't want to be in a group with these four fabulous girls instead of us boring old boys? I mean, seriously—I know it's no contest!" The boys laughed, and Cloe looked relieved. She hadn't meant to cause any problems between her guy friends!

"So you were just hanging around because you were into the whole cooking thing?" she asked.

"Well . . . yeah," Eitan admitted. "And you are my friends, and you needed my help, so I helped. But I definitely did *not* give Jade the wrong flour!" he added.

"Geez, Eitan, I'm sorry," Cloe said. "You really were just trying to help, and here I accuse you of ruining our recipe!"

"It's cool," he said. "I was acting like a total idiot, so I don't blame you for suspecting me."

"Thanks, man," Cloe said. "I really appreciate you being so chill about it. But now I'd better jet—we still have a culprit to catch!"

Chapter 7

When Cloe got back to Yasmin's place, the girls couldn't wait to get the whole story. But they were totally disappointed when they learned the mystery still wasn't solved—though they were really glad that their friend Eitan hadn't messed them up on purpose!

"Okay then, if we got everything on the ingredient list, and followed the recipe exactly, then all that leaves is that the recipe was wrong," Sasha concluded.

"There's no way Louis Lyle's recipe was wrong!" Yasmin cried.

"But what if the version of it we had *was*?" Jade asked.

"Do you mean—?" Cloe asked.

"Well, I know Kiana's a huge Louis Lyle fan too," Jade said. "I mean, she's gotta be if she has all his books, right? So I mean, it *is* possible that she copied it down wrong to throw us off."

"That's so mean though!" Yasmin exclaimed. "Do you really think she would do something like that?"

"I don't want to think so," Jade said, "but it seems like the obvious answer."

Just then, Yasmin let out a huge yawn. "I'm with Yas," Cloe said. "It's late, and we can get the scoop from Kiana tomorrow. For now, let's get our beauty sleep, 'kay?"

"Totally," the girls agreed. But they all worried that they wouldn't sleep well until they knew what had gone wrong with their perfect meal!

* * *

The next day at school, Sasha waited eagerly for Kiana to come into first lesson. She couldn't wait to confront her!

"Hey, girl," Kiana said, taking a seat next to Sasha. "How's it going?"

"Well, I mean, we're all still pretty upset about the baking fiasco yesterday," Sasha said.

"Yeah, that totally sucked," Kiana agreed.

"You know what else sucked?" Sasha demanded. "That *somebody* gave us the wrong recipe!"

Kiana looked shocked, and Sasha felt bad—she knew she could be harsh sometimes, but Yasmin was totally crushed and she was determined to get to the bottom of this!

"You don't really think *I* had anything to do with this, do you?" Kiana asked.

"Well, you did give us the recipe, and you were on an opposing team," Sasha said. "And I'm sorry to have to accuse you, but you're the only one who could've done it."

"But I didn't!" Kiana cried. "I'd never do something like that to you guys, and I can prove it! Do you still have the recipe card I gave you?"

"Of course," Sasha replied. "It's evidence."

"Great," Kiana said. "Because I have the book right here, so you'll see they're a perfect match!" She pulled her Louis Lyle cookbook out of her book bag and opened it to the pumpernickel bread recipe. Sasha dug through her bag for the index card, and handed it over. Together, they went through it line by line, and couldn't find one thing wrong.

"But I don't understand," Sasha said. "You were the only one left who could've done it. I'm really sorry I suspected you—but now I don't know what to think!"

"Maybe you should talk to Louis Lyle," Kiana suggested. "He's the guest speaker in Ms. Shepard's second lesson, and I think she was making him a gourmet breakfast in her classroom first. You could probably catch them there."

"That's a spectacular idea!" Sasha exclaimed. "Kiana, I can't believe you're still helping me after I just totally accused you!"

"Hey, you're my friend," Kiana said. "And I understand, you were just protecting Yasmin. It's okay."

"Thanks so much!" Sasha said, giving her friend a quick hug. "Now I'd better get a move on!" She darted to the front of the classroom, book and recipe card in hand, and begged the teacher for a hall pass. After she explained the situation, he agreed, and she bolted for Ms. Shepard's classroom. She didn't want to miss her last chance to set things right!

Chapter 8

"Ms. Shepard, Ms. Shepard!" Sasha called, bursting into the cooking classroom. Her teacher looked up, startled, from the omelette she was preparing.

"My goodness, Sasha, what's wrong?" she asked.

"I know Yasmin didn't make the bread wrong," Sasha said. "It wasn't her fault!" Ms. Shepard looked unsure, so Sasha thrust the book and index card at her. "Here, look—they're exactly the same!"

Ms. Shepard looked back and forth

between the two, still keeping an eye on her omelette. "Yes, they do seem to match, but I don't understand what that proves."

"Oh hello, Sasha, good to see you again," Chef Lyle said, stepping out of Ms. Shepard's office. "What brings you here?"

"Can you please look at this cookbook?" she said. "I think there might be a mistake in it."

He took the book from her and shook his head. "Ah, it's one of mine—I'm sure there's nothing wrong in here. I wrote all of these recipes myself!" He read through the list of ingredients, nodding as he went. "Then there's dark rye flour, wholewheat flour, cracked wheat flour, brown rice flour—wait, *not* brown rice flour!"

"What?" Ms. Shepard asked, shocked.

"Rice flour makes bread really crumbly— this is supposed to be buckwheat flour, which helps bread stick together," he explained.

"But how could it have gotten in there?" Ms. Shepard asked.

"Well, I was playing around with a wheat-free version of this recipe," Louis began. "My sister has a wheat allergy, and I wanted her to be able to try my favourite bread. But this never should've made it into the cookbook like this—the whole recipe would need to be adjusted for it to work with this type of flour!"

"Oh my goodness," Ms. Shepard said. "So Yasmin really did follow the recipe correctly. It's the recipe that was wrong!"

"Sasha, thank you so much for finding this

mistake," Louis Lyle said. "I'll have to have my publisher do a reprint immediately. I just feel so bad that millions of my fans might have been making my bread wrong all this time!"

"I know what we could do about that," Sasha said slyly.

Chapter 9

Sasha, Cloe, Yasmin and Jade couldn't believe they were standing in a real celebrity chef's kitchen, about to cook one of his specialties in front of millions of viewers! At their sides were Eitan and Kiana, who Sasha had asked to join them as an apology for suspecting them. And not only were the girls on Louis's show, but he was doing an hour-long special so he could explain about the recipe mix-up, and then they could all demonstrate how to make his scrumptious bread the right way. Today, they were the stars of the show!

"This is even cooler than I thought it

would be!" whispered Jade as she, Cloe, Yasmin, Sasha, Eitan and Kiana waited backstage at Louis's TV studio. They'd gotten to be on the taping at their school too, along with the guys, but then Louis had flown them out to his own studio as an extra thank you!

"Totally! We're like celebrities!" said Sasha.

"Well, that's just as it should be!" Yasmin said, and they all burst into giggles.

They were listening to Louis taping his opening out front, explaining about the recipe mix-up and how his guests today had solved the mystery, when Ms. Shepard appeared backstage. "Okay, that's your cue. Get out onstage and show all those wannabe chefs out there that Stiles High chefs are the absolute best!"

The girls and Eitan ran towards the stage just as Louis announced, "And now, I'd like to welcome my special guests today, the coolest chefs I know—Sasha, Jade, Yasmin, Cloe, Eitan and Kiana!" Ms. Shepard applauded wildly along with the audience as her students made their way onstage.

"So today, we're going to replicate the meal these fine young chefs made for me," Louis continued, "only this time the recipe will be absolutely perfect—just like their cooking skills!"

"Now, let's get to work. First things first, every proper chef needs a hat." With that, Ms. Shepard brought out six chef hats for each of them to wear. Each one was personalized with their names embroidered on the brim.

"Sweet!" exclaimed Eitan as he placed it on his head.

"Super-stylin'!" Jade agreed.

"Sasha, let's get started," said Louis. "Start chopping the celery. Cloe and Jade, you start mixing the mayonnaise and the honey. Eitan, you go ahead and dump the curry into the mixture."

They all got to work, and Louis pulled Yasmin and Kiana over to a separate countertop. "Girls, you'll be helping me on what is, as you know, the very hardest part of this meal—baking the pumpernickel bread!"

Louis looked straight into the camera with a wry smile. "Now keep an eye on me, faithful viewers—don't let me botch this one again!" The girls laughed—they loved that even though he was so famous and talented, Louis totally wasn't afraid to make fun of himself! Soon they were all baking busily, and in no time at all, the salad was prepared and Louis was taking the loaves of bread out of the oven.

"Things sure go faster on television!" Jade whispered to Yasmin.

"I know, it's like magic!" Yasmin replied.

"Okay, here we are," said Louis. "We have a delicious curried-chicken salad on home-made pumpernickel bread. Warm, delicious and perfect for any luncheon, no matter what the occasion."

"Hey, Yasmin, take a little taste of this bread and tell me what you think!" said Louis.

Yasmin cautiously sampled the bread as everyone else looked on anxiously. *Please, please let this be right!* thought Yasmin, crossing her fingers for good luck.

She chewed, swallowed and grinned. "So good!" she exclaimed.

"Phew!" said Louis. "It's amazing how important every little ingredient is, isn't it?"

"No doubt!" Yasmin agreed.

"And that's it for today," said Louis, smiling for the camera. "Thanks for joining me and remember—play with your food, cuz food is fun!"

"And cut!" yelled the director.

Sasha, Jade, Eitan, Kiana, Cloe and Yasmin rushed into a huge group hug. "That was so amazin'!" said Jade. "We rule!"

"Hey, what about me?" asked Louis. "I

mean, I *am* the famous chef here—don't I rule too?"

"Totally!" the girls exclaimed, laughing, as they pulled Louis and their teacher into their group hug too. Ms. Shepard looked surprised, but soon she was hugging right along with them.

"That was a great show, everybody," Louis said. "You're welcome back anytime. But now, it's time for the best part of any cooking show—let's eat!"

They all cheered as they rushed to try out the meal they'd just prepared, and were thrilled to discover that it was absolutely perfect!